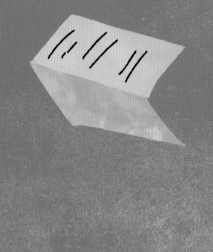

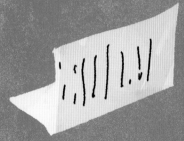
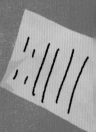

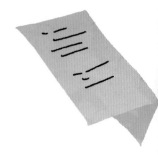

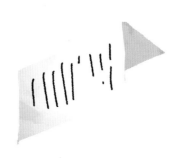

FOR MY PARENTS —H.K.R.

FOR KATRINA, LILY, MAX, AND COLIN. I LOVE YOU. —P.C.

Text copyright © 2020 by Helena Ku Rhee
Jacket art and interior illustrations copyright © 2020 by Pascal Campion

All rights reserved. Published in the United States by Random House Children's Books,
a division of Penguin Random House LLC, New York.

Random House and the colophon are registered trademarks of Penguin Random House LLC.

Visit us on the Web!
rhcbooks.com

Educators and librarians, for a variety of teaching tools, visit us at RHTeachersLibrarians.com

Library of Congress Cataloging-in-Publication Data is available upon request.
ISBN 978-0-525-64461-3 (trade) — ISBN 978-0-525-64462-0 (lib. bdg.) — ISBN 978-0-525-64463-7 (ebook)

MANUFACTURED IN CHINA
10 9 8 7 6 5 4 3 2 1
First Edition

Random House Children's Books supports the First Amendment and celebrates the right to read.

THE
PAPER KINGDOM

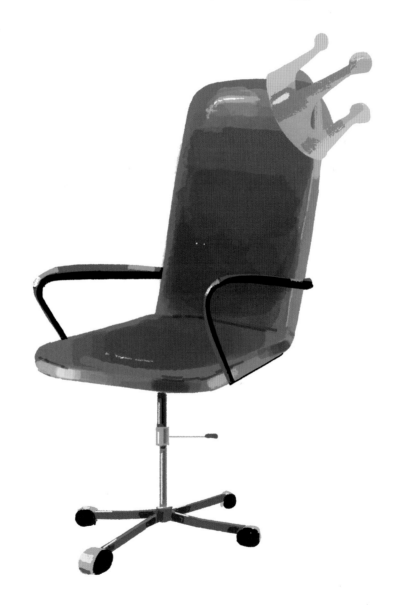

by
HELENA KU RHEE

illustrated by
PASCAL CAMPION

RANDOM HOUSE 🏠 NEW YORK

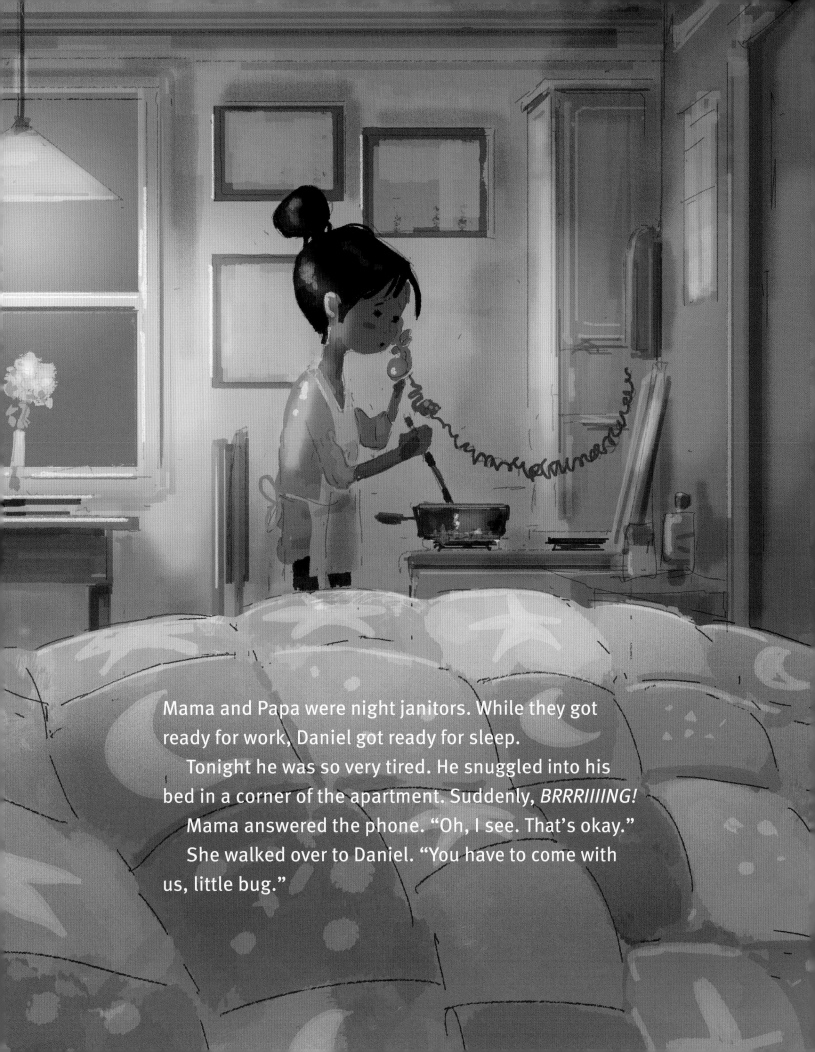

Mama and Papa were night janitors. While they got
ready for work, Daniel got ready for sleep.
    Tonight he was so very tired. He snuggled into his
bed in a corner of the apartment. Suddenly, *BRRRIIIING!*
    Mama answered the phone. "Oh, I see. That's okay."
    She walked over to Daniel. "You have to come with
us, little bug."

"Too sleepy, Mama. I'll wait for Auntie Clara."

"That was Clara. She can't come tonight."

"Can I stay upstairs with Dwayne's family?"

"No, we ask them for too many favors,"
Papa said.

"Then I'll stay here by myself. I'll be good."

Papa shook his head and helped Daniel
change out of his pajamas.

Their old car sputtered as they drove
to Mama and Papa's work downtown.

The big glass building always looked angry.
It seemed to say "Stay out!"
    "Can't I just sleep in the car?" Daniel asked.

But Mama and Papa said no. They hurried Daniel inside and waved at Sam, the security guard.

"Hello, Daniel!" said Sam. "Wow, you've grown! Soon you'll be as tall as me!"

Daniel doubted he'd grow to be a giant like Sam.

"I won't tell anyone he's here." Sam winked at Mama and Papa.

"Thank you, Sam," Papa said as they got in the elevator.

Daniel was so tired he felt like crying. "When can we leave?"

Mama and Papa didn't answer. From a big closet, they got brooms, mops, sprays, vacuums, and buckets. So many tools!

Daniel sneezed. "Why's that stuff so dirty?"

"Because they keep the kingdom clean," said Mama.

Daniel was confused. "What kingdom?"

"The Paper Kingdom," Papa said. "Didn't we tell you before? This is the land of the Paper King!"

"The Paper King?" Now Daniel felt awake. "How come I never saw him? Where is he?"

"Let's go see," Mama said. "Maybe he's in his throne room."
They went to a large room with a desk as long as a banquet table in a castle. A tall chair stood behind the desk.
"Looks like the king's gone to bed," said Papa. "Let's clean up for him."

Mama picked up paper from the floor. Papa emptied the wastebasket.

"Why so much paper?" Daniel asked.

"It's the Paper Kingdom, remember?" said Papa. "The king checks all the paper, and if anything has a mistake, out it goes!"

Papa vacuumed. Sometimes
he stopped to wipe his forehead.

"But why do
you have to clean
the kingdom?"
Daniel asked.

Mama dusted.
She sneezed as
she worked.

"Shhhh!" said Mama, looking around.
"Don't upset the queen."
"Where is she?"

Papa led Daniel into the
hallway. "She's usually over
there, and she's the busiest
of all. She sends paper to
everyone in the kingdom."

Mama dusted the queen's shelves.

Daniel took a canister from Mama's cart to water the queen's plant.

"Let's check out the bathroom," Papa said.

"I don't have to go yet," said Daniel.

"I know," said Papa. "But let's make sure dragons aren't hiding there."

"Dragons?" Daniel scooted behind Papa.

"Oh, don't worry. They work for the king," Papa said. "They're small and friendly, but sometimes they hide because they're afraid."

"Of what?" Daniel asked.

"The king," said Papa. "And maybe the queen."

When they got to the bathroom, Daniel was glad
no dragons were there. Papa cleaned each stall.
"Maybe they're in the kitchen," Papa said.
"Dragons love to eat!"

The kitchen was dark and quiet. "Smart dragons," said Mama. "Guess they won't get caught today."

Papa turned on the light. The kitchen was a disaster! Mama wiped spills and picked up trash.

Papa swept the floor and straightened tables and chairs. Sometimes Papa rubbed his neck and Mama sneezed.

"Why are dragons so messy?" asked Daniel. "They should pick up their own trash!"

Mama said, "Maybe they ate in a rush and forgot to clean up. They don't mean to be naughty."

"But why do *you* have to clean it all?" It made Daniel hurt inside to see Mama and Papa clean such a huge mess by themselves. "Not fair! I'm going to yell at the dragons!" He angrily threw a banana peel in the trash.

"No, little bug. Only the king can yell at dragons," Mama said. "You know what that means?"

Daniel shrugged.

"Someday you'll have to be king!"
Papa smiled. "Then you can sit in the
throne room and tell the dragons to be
nice and neat."

Daniel liked the sound
of that. "Can I see the
throne room again?"

Daniel sat in the tall chair. He closed
his eyes and imagined a kingdom with
small dragons who picked up their
litter. In the castle, papers were piled
high. In the throne room, the chair
seemed to reach the sky.

"Remember, little bug," Mama whispered.
"Remember to be nice when you become king.
The dragons work hard too." She hummed as
she wiped the windows.

Daniel didn't realize they were home until he felt Mama tuck him in. He snuggled into his bed in a corner of the apartment. He thought about the Paper Kingdom. He decided if he became king someday, he wouldn't yell at the little dragons, but he'd make sure they cleaned their mess. That way, Mama and Papa wouldn't have to.

AUTHOR'S NOTE

My parents worked as night janitors in a corporate building when I was little. On nights they couldn't find a relative or friend to watch me, they took me with them to work. I have vague memories of dozing on office chairs while my parents mopped, swept, and vacuumed. And to keep my grumpiness at bay, they told funny stories about the people who worked in the offices during the day. My parents used their humor and imagination to make an unpleasant situation seem full of possibility and magic. I wrote *The Paper Kingdom* for them, and for all hardworking families.